I ♥ YOU

Always with You, Always with Me

Written by KELLY ROWLAND and JESSICA McKAY
Illustrated by FANNY LIEM

VIKING

Monday

My darling child, there is a part of the day that your eyes never see.
It's the wee hours of the morning, when it's time to start a new week.
Before I go building at work, Mommy builds your world!

Breakfast ✓
Lunch ✓
Permission Slip ✓
Karate Uniform ✓
Monday Motivation ✓
"We Got This!"

cereal

Then, as if perfectly choreographed by the universe itself, you, the sun, and the birds all rise and greet me with your light.

"Good morning, Mommy!" you say with a smile.

But your smile quickly disappears.
"What's wrong, my love?" I ask.
"It's Monday. That means you have to go to work," you say, on the verge of tears.

"Honey, I know it's hard. I miss you when I'm at work, too. But remember, you are the most important thing in my life! Be on the lookout for magic traces throughout the day to show we're never too far apart."
Suddenly your eyes light up with excitement.

Later at school, you find my magic traces and hear the words I always say:

When I leave for work, you may think I'm not around,
But if you look closely, you'll see I can be found.
Traces of magic here and there
Show that we are an inseparable pair.
Always with you,
Always with me,
Mommy and child
Together we'll be.

Tuesday

Today I'm on a business trip. I march onto the site where we will be breaking ground and smile as I envision my design coming to life.

As I work, I see your magic traces.

That gets me thinking that I can't wait to see what you'll be when you grow up!

I hope you will remember the words I say to you:
When I leave for work, you may think I'm not around,
But if you look closely, you'll see I can be found.
Traces of magic here and there
Show that we are an inseparable pair.
Always with you,
Always with me,
Mommy and child
Together we'll be.

Wednesday

I love when you surprise me with a phone call! You and Daddy seem to be having a lot of fun. Remember, today is Waffle Wednesday at Auntie's house after Daddy goes to work. I miss you so much and can't wait to see you tomorrow when I'm back from my trip.

Before you know it, I think you'll forget that you even miss me.

But at bedtime you say, "I miss my mommy."

"Don't worry," Auntie replies. "She's just one night's sleep away. Until then, I'll tuck you in with the blanket she made for you."

And just like that, you feel my magic traces:

When I leave for work, you may think I'm not around,
But if you look closely, you'll see I can be found.
Traces of magic here and there
Show that we are an inseparable pair.
Always with you,
Always with me,
Mommy and child
Together we'll be.

Thursday

Today I come home and we go on a fun field trip! As we walk through the museum, I love seeing the exhibit and the world through your eyes.

Soon it's time for me to go.
"Mommy, why can't I go with you?" you cry. "The other kids are going home with their parents! It's not fair!"

"Sweetie, I have to go back to work. But don't worry, we'll have dinner together. Then at bedtime I'll read your favorite story. Remember my magic words, and I'll see you tonight," I say.

As the bus drives away, I see your magic traces.

When I leave for work, you may think I'm not around,
But if you look closely, you'll see I can be found.
Traces of magic here and there
Show that we are an inseparable pair.
Always with you,
Always with me,
Mommy and child
Together we'll be.

Friday

You wake up not feeling well, which means we won't be leaving the house today. But work doesn't stop for the sniffles. I'll work from home while you rest, and sneak upstairs for extra kisses and hugs until you're feeling your best!

As I leave your room, I whisper the magic words:

When I leave for work, you may think I'm not around,
But if you look closely, you'll see I can be found.
Traces of magic here and there
Show that we are an inseparable pair.
Always with you,
Always with me,
Mommy and child
Together we'll be.

JAM
COCOA
SALT

Saturday

Time for pancakes and pajamas! Turn on the music! Let's jam.

I'll grab the ingredients. Flour, sugar, and milk, with a side of silly faces, a pinch of your chubby cheeks, and lots of love. Voilà! The pancakes are ready for our favorite part . . . the bubbles!

We sit and watch the batter bubble.
Doing this with you never gets old!

Once the pancakes have been poured, flipped, and drizzled, we get cozy on the couch and catch up all morning long . . . together.

Today I won't leave for work, and I will be around,
No matter what, I can be found.
The magic in the air
Shows that we are an inseparable pair.
Always with you,
Always with me,
Mommy and child
Together we'll be.

Sunday

The days go by so fast, and before we know it, it's a new week again.

As we head to bed tonight, let's say these words together:

Tomorrow you'll leave for work, and I'll think you're not around,
But if I look closely, I'll see you can be found.
Traces of magic here and there
Show that we are an inseparable pair.
Always with you,
Always with me,
Mommy and child
Together we'll be.

For Titan and Noah, I do it all for you! —K. R.

For my parents, who modeled the work/family juggle with grace, as well as the generations of working mothers and fathers in my family before them. And for my three beautiful children and amazing husband, who ride this roller coaster called life with me. Mommy is always with you. —J. M.

VIKING
An imprint of Penguin Random House LLC, New York

First published in the United States of America by Viking,
an imprint of Penguin Random House LLC, 2022

Published in cooperation with Hightree Publishing

Library of Congress Cataloging-in-Publication Data is available.

Printed in the United States of America

ISBN 9780593465516

10 9 8 7 6 5 4 3 2 1

PC

Text set in Caecilia

I ♥ YOU
I ♥ YOU